Town house, Country House

illustrated by Jess Stockham

Child's Play (International) Ltd
Ashworth Rd, Bridgemead, Swindon, SN5 7YD UK
Swindon   Auburn MF   Sydney
© 2012 Child's Play (International) Ltd   Printed in

Once upon a time, there was a little mouse.
She lived in a field in the country,
cleverly hidden in a small nest of straw.

One summer's day, she sent a postcard to her cousin, who lived in the big town along the road.

To
Town Mouse
Mousetown
CH3 3SE

"Please come and visit me," she wrote. "It's lovely here in the countryside! We can have a picnic in the sunshine, and go swimming in the river! Do come!"

The town mouse read the postcard excitedly.
"What a good idea!" he exclaimed. "I need a change
from the big city. It's so big and noisy and dirty!
Some fresh air and healthy food will be good for me!"

To
Town Mouse
Mousetown
CH3 3SE

TAIL
SPINNER

The country mouse welcomed her cousin with a hug.
"Welcome to the country!" she smiled.
"You're just in time for lunch!"
"That's great!" he answered. "I'm starving!"

The two mice climbed a branch, and the country
mouse showed the town mouse how to find nuts
and berries in the trees and bushes. The town mouse
picked the largest nut and biggest berry he could find.

All of a sudden, he pulled a face.
"Ugh!" he said. "These nuts are really dry,
and the berries are really bitter!
Can't we have some sugar on them?"
"They taste fine to me," answered the country mouse.
"And what's sugar?"

"Shall we swim instead?" suggested the town mouse. They jumped into the river, but the town mouse jumped out again straight away.
"What's the matter?" cried the country mouse.

"It's freezing!" he shivered.
"Can't you heat it?"

"No!" laughed his cousin. "It's a river, not a pool!
Perhaps we should go for a walk."
The two mice set off along the rocky path
by the side of the river. They had not gone very
far before the town mouse sat down again.
"It's too hot!" he said. "And the path is too muddy
and uneven. How much further do we have to walk?"

"We don't have to walk at all,"
answered the country mouse.
"What would you like to do instead?"
"I'm not sure," said her cousin. "There's not much
to do in the country at all! Shall we just rest in
this field for a little while?" They found some shade
underneath a tree, and sat down in the long grass.
"This is the life!" said the town mouse,
beginning to fall asleep.

But all of a sudden, a head poked over the stone wall and let out a very loud MOOOOOOOOOOOOO!

"What on earth was that?!"
the town mouse cried, shivering with fear.
"Don't be frightened!" said the country mouse, trying not to laugh. "It's only a cow! There are lots of them in the country! It won't bother us!"

That night, the two mice curled up in the nest.
"I can't sleep!" moaned the town mouse. "This straw bed is too itchy! You know, I'm not sure I like it here after all. The food is a bit dull, and the river's too cold. You have to walk everywhere, and those cows are downright dangerous! Why don't you come with me to the city? It's much better than the country. There's so much to do, and plenty of fantastic food! You'll love it!"
"It does sound exciting," agreed his cousin. "Maybe I do need a change. Why don't we set off now?"

When the two mice arrived in town,
they went straight to the town mouse's home.
They climbed through a little hole cut into the wall.
"Make yourself at home!" said the town mouse.
"I'll go and find us some supper!"

"I'm tired after the journey," thought the country mouse. "I'll just have a little nap."
She sat on a soft velvet chair, and fell into a deep sleep. But all of a sudden there was a terrible roar!

She sat up, listening. Then there was another roar!
"What on earth is that?" she wondered.
"I wish my cousin were here!"
She climbed out of the chair, and hid in a dusty corner until the town mouse came back.

The town mouse squeezed in through the hole with his arms full of the finest foods. "Look what I found!" he cried. "Cakes, biscuits, cheese and ham and – where are you?!"

The country mouse crawled out of the corner. "There was a loud noise that scared me," she explained. "I thought the roof was going to fall in. There it is again!"

"Oh, you mustn't worry about that!" laughed her cousin. "It's only a train! They rattle past every hour or so! But they're as harmless as cows!"

The town mouse spread a silk cloth over the table, and they sat down to the fabulous feast.
The country mouse was hungry, but she stopped eating before long.

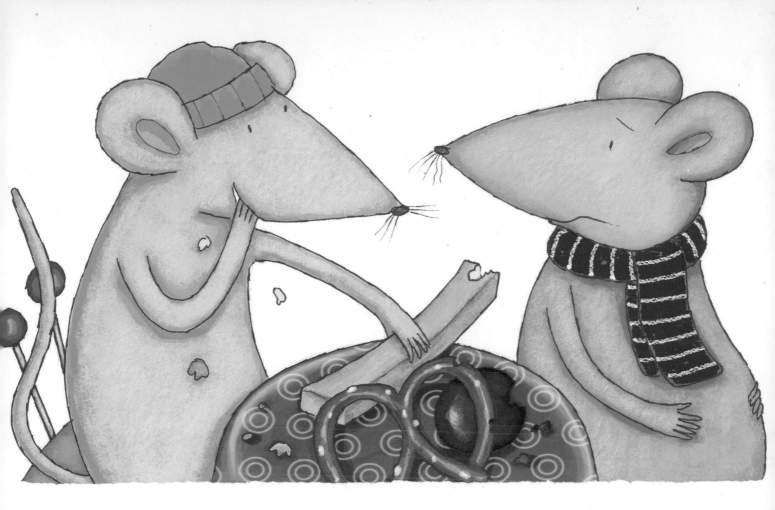

"What's the matter?" asked her cousin. "Not hungry?"
"It's very nice," replied the country mouse.
"It's much grander than the food I eat at home,
but it's very...rich. I can't eat too much of it
without feeling sick."
"Suit yourself!" said the town mouse. "I'll finish yours!"

After supper, the country mouse
wanted some exercise.
"Shall we go for a walk now?" she asked.
"No one walks in the city," answered the town mouse.
"I'm going to teach you to skateboard!
And you can meet the cat!"
They crept out into a massive room full of furniture.

"Pussy Cat, Pussy Cat!" he shouted. "Where are you?
Yoo-hoo! You can't catch me!"
In an instant, there was a terrible wail,
and a large ball of fur appeared!
"Skate!" shouted the town mouse.
"Skate for your life!"

The cat chased them around the room
and behind the flowers! It chased them
under the table and over the sofa!

They knocked over vases and pictures.
They ran across the table, and scattered
cake crumbs everywhere.

"Time for a rest!" shouted the town mouse. "Quickly, in here!" And he dragged his cousin back into the mouse hole.

As she fell asleep that night in the feather bed
her cousin had made for her, the country mouse
thought of the home she had left behind. She missed
the fields, the hedges and the river. She missed
the simple berries and nuts. She missed the sheep
and the noisy cows.

The next morning, she explained to her cousin that she was homesick, and that it was time to leave for home. "That was fun!" he said, wiping his brow with a fine handkerchief. "Isn't the town exciting?!"

"Maybe," replied the country mouse. "But maybe it's a little too exciting! Thank you so much for the visit, but I think it's time for me to go home now. I'm a country mouse at heart, and the country is where I belong!"